The Crooked Forest

Beyond

Written and illustrated by
Joni Franks

To order additional copies of this book, contact:
Xlibris
844-714-8691
www.Xlibris.com
Orders@Xlibris.com

ISBN: Softcover   979-8-3694-2540-4
        Hardcover   979-8-3694-2541-1
        EBook   979-8-3694-2542-8

Library of Congress Control Number: 2024914256

Print information available on the last page

Rev. date: 07/15/2024

Books by Joni Franks

Corky Tails: Tales of a Tailless Dog Named Sagebrush Book Series:
Corky Tails
Sagebrush Meets the Shuns
Sagebrush and the Smoke Jumper
Sagebrush and the Butterfly Creek Flood
Sagebrush and the Warm Springs Discovery
Rabos Taponados
Corky Tails Coloring Book
Sagebrush and the Disappearing Dark Sky
Sagebrush and the Never Summer Mountains
Holly Berry and Mistletoe

The Crooked Forest Book Series
The Crooked Forest, Legacy of the Holey Stone
The Crooked Forest, Cloud Crazed
The Crooked Forest, Beyond

Heart Songs

Beyond ~ something that lies just outside the scope of ordinary experience.

Everything is alive
Nothing truly dies
Shifting into changing forms
Wandering far and wide

Interweaving lives like vines
Creating unique storylines
Planting seeds early on
Growing roots forming bonds

Creations blowing in the breeze
Living life as they please
Before this flash in time is gone
And has slipped into the great beyond

The Betwixt and Between Place

She had traveled this familiar path before, by day and by night, awake and in her dreams. As Wynter returned to the betwixt and between place, where the two paths crossed, she recollected the day when she had arrived here. Now the seasons of the past year seemed to have passed as quickly as just a few days, and Wynter sensed that the betwixt and between place might be a slightly dangerous place to linger.

Wynter had been safely tucked away for the past one year and one day, oblivious to the outside world and the storm that was currently brewing within the Crooked Forest. The atmosphere was becoming unstable, and the wind was escalating in intensity as the eerie yellow clouds grew and spread across the entire sky.

This gloomy weather was in utter contrast to Wynter's hopeful mood. During her time away, she had recovered from a heart-breaking life experience. Today, she felt lighter as she returned to this supernatural place, where no rules or obligations exist. Even the marriage law was suspended here. She was free to do as she pleased.

The winds escalated and Wynter pulled the hood of her bright purple cloak onto her head, noting that the air felt exceptionally hot and humid. The clouds were becoming darker, signaling the power they contained. Sudden blasts of warm air nearly ripped Wynter's cloak from her body, and dirt and grit obscured her vision as she struggled to stand upright. She had to find shelter.

Fast-moving thunderstorms accompanied by a line of straight-line winds were creating a violent tempest known as a derecho that strikes without warning. This storm spawned tornadoes, heavy rain, hail, and hurricane force gusts that wreaked havoc upon the Crooked Forest, changing the landscape of the forest forever as well as altering the lives of all beings who called the Crooked Forest home.

There's hurt within this painful place
Where the crack runs through my heart
I'm searching for a new home base
New beginnings and fresh starts

Wild Magic

There are places in the woodlands that are filled with magic so wild and so powerful that a sense of awe is felt there. Snowdonia was such a place. Throughout the ages, the trees, rocks, and streams in Snowdonia had remained hidden and mostly untouched by human activity.

Wynter had spent the last one year and one day in Snowdonia. There, she had faithfully practiced a daily ritual, patiently waiting to see what would be revealed to her. Through tolerance, she had endured a year and one day of total isolation. She had completely withdrawn from society and pursued no new endeavors until the bleakness of her heart pain passed.

The purpose of the yearlong ritual was to immerse Wynter totally in the experience without distraction, connecting her to the power of nature, enabling her to question, ponder, and conclude her transformation. In Snowdonia, Wynter experienced nature's remedy by carefully following the instructions imparted to her by May Fae, the fairy.

She had gathered herbs, roots, and plants each day and throughout the seasons, adding each ingredient to the boiling water of the magical cauldron just as she had been instructed.

Each month's mix was then added to the previous month's brew. The sacred herbs, roots, and flowers cast their magic, and Wynter accessed the mystery of the cauldron by drinking the brew after one year and one day had passed.

"I have added the roots while stirring the flowers. May the magical cauldron help in revealing my power," Wynter recited boldly.

She also practiced the custom of visibly wearing willow as an emblem of the emotional turmoil she felt inside. She gathered willow branches and patiently weaved them into a small bracelet that she never took off until her final day in Snowdonia, when she consumed the concoction and removed the willow bracelet from her wrist, flinging it into the hot flames that flickered under the magical cauldron's belly, watching as it disintegrated.

Now it had been over a year since Wynter had fled from her husband, Aidan, and the life they had built together in the village of New Leaf. It was only by accident that she learned that her husband had not been honest with her about his real identity.

The truth arrived unexpectedly one morning while Wynter was tending her vegetable garden and overheard the whisperings of her neighbors next door. The neighbor ladies suspected that Wynter's husband was the very person responsible for the drought that had recently occurred in the nearby village of Flowerville.

The women spoke of how Aidan had angered Dewdrop, the elemental water fairy that watched over Sleeping Creek, by hatching a scheme to divert water from Sleeping Creek into Dragonfly Ditch since Dragonfly Ditch wasn't providing enough water for the village of Flowerville.

The truth was that Aidan wanted to be considered a human hero and a great and powerful magician, capable of diverting the water of Sleeping Creek by simply asking the water to move. But Aidan was not a magician at all. Armed with a pick and a shovel, Aidan dug a trench alongside Sleeping Creek until finally the pristine waters broke through, and the diversion trench channeled the precious water into Dragonfly Ditch.

Instantly Dewdrop appeared and promptly halted the water diversion scheme. In the blink of a fairy's eye, Dragonfly Ditch dried up and the village of Flowerville was stricken with drought. Prosperity and joy were no longer found in Flowerville. It became a pocket of stagnation, where little energy flowed, rendering it a dead zone for the next seven generations to come.

Because of Aidan's actions, life became harder than it ever needed to be for all beings in and around Flowerville. Aidan and his flock of sheep suffered terribly as water was scarce, and great distances had to be traversed to find sufficient water for himself and his sheep.

The residents of Flowerville dispersed in all directions after losing Dragonfly Ditch, traveling over the nearby hills and knolls searching for another source of water.

Wynter recalled the day when she first met Aidan. She was in the Crooked Forest near the budding village of New Leaf where many were building huts after fleeing Flowerville.

Aidan and Wynter stood together on a high ridge as she pointed out the new village springing up beside a tributary of Sleeping Creek where she wished to make her home.

"The reason I am here is because of a man that had no respect for nature or the elemental beings. Due to his reckless behavior, I lost my home, and Flowerville lost its precious water source, Dragonfly Ditch," Wynter conveyed to Aidan.

"I have never met the man that was the cause of the environmental atrocity, but I certainly know that I would not want anything to do with such a person," Wynter continued.

Aidan shifted nervously from one foot to the other.

"Can you blame me?" Wynter questioned Aidan.

Aidan felt the fleeting opportunity to speak the truth and admit that he was the man she spoke of, but he was not that brave.

"No, Miss, I cannot," Aidan lied.

And that is precisely when the trouble between Aidan and Wynter began.

Within the dark forest
There once lived a hare
As swift as the eagle
Who glides through the air
No legend no song
Or folktale compares
To the story of Kai
The magical hare

Kai

Within the Crooked Forest lived shapeshifting hares that could transform into fairies at will. These nature spirits were as timeless as the wind and the rain and often carried messages from the Otherworld where they came and went from as they pleased.

Hares are natural burrowers and live deep within maze-like tunnels, signifying their deep connection with earth energy. They have large ears and are good listeners, and they possess sharp alert senses that make them adept at spotting danger. Hares can run more than forty miles per hour and can jump up to ten feet in the air. The traits of the hare are known to be useful in situations where adaptability is needed or a quick change of direction is required to avoid disaster. They teach us that by staying alert and sensing which way the wind is blowing, one can avoid danger.

The name Kai means holder to the key to the earth, and Kai's mysterious underground world was reached by traveling through the mists, hills, wetlands, and trees, as there are no sealed passages between the landscapes of the middle world, and Kai's home in the Otherworld.

Kai stood on his long hind legs, sniffing the air, instinctively detecting that someone nearby was in distress, possibly disoriented in the derecho, and in need of his assistance. Springing into action, he began his quest to find that individual and assist them as the violent storm gained intensity.

Samhain

pronounced *sawin*

An ancient celebration that marks the beginning of winter and the new year. Celebrated from October 31 to November 1 when the barriers between the physical world and the spirit world are believed to break down and supernatural episodes can occur.

Lost in this wild place on the night of Samhain
Further away from where I have been

Colorful leaves embracing the breeze
Laughing fairies call out to me

The singing Hawthorn draws me in
Requesting that I enter its den

Beyond

Wynter had traveled beyond the betwixt and between place. There were no defined paths, just an ancient trek way system to navigate. Clasping her bright purple cloak tightly around her shoulders, she carefully stepped over the fallen trees in her path.

Wynter hoped she would not become lost in this wild place where the energy felt intense and the trees were tangled and intertwined, their roots becoming one and a part of each other.

Wynter was about to enter another realm where strange things that are considered to happen only in dreams would now occur during waking hours and in broad daylight. She was about to walk through an invisible doorway, where the familiar rules of time and space no longer apply. This world was beyond the understanding she had of nature itself, and the good forces that dwell there that can easily shift reality.

Secret entrances are often found in tree trunks and openings in the ground, and the thorny seven-hundred-year-old Hawthorn tree in Wynter's path held an undefinable otherworldly energy that drew her to it. She watched as eyes appeared in the tree trunk. It was as if the tree was watching her. Little did she know that this ancient tree housed a hidden world under its massive root system that had occupied this space for centuries.

The ancient tree was really two Hawthorn trees that had twisted around each other and now grew as one, looking as if they were embracing each other. Studying the tree, Wynter reflected on her marriage to Aidan. She wished with all her heart that she and Aidan's life together had evolved like these two strong and sturdy ones. The two trees had grabbed onto each other with such a strong and determined life force that they had become one.

Looking up into the highest branches of the tree, Wynter saw mistletoe growing abundantly, attaching itself to the tree's spiny branches. Mistletoe, the white-berried, medicinal plant was known to cure disease and ease intense headaches and was favored for its all healing qualities.

From the corner of her eye, Wynter spied Kai, the magical hare, watching her intently, staring deeply into her eyes.

Wynter gasped with surprise at the sudden appearance of the hare.

"Look out!" Kai screamed above the moaning wind, as a tall dead tree cracked at its base, falling to the ground, missing Wynter by mere inches.

"Follow me!" Kai screamed as he led Wynter to his grassy nest tucked away at the base of where the two twisted trees grew together as one. This secret entrance had existed for eons, even prior to the time when ice covered the land.

Running as fast as she could to keep up, Wynter watched as Kai dropped through the mound of soft earth at the base of the tree. Following closely behind, Wynter never once thought about how she might ever get out of this place again. Effortlessly she leaped through the soft mossy spot, landing in a soft bed of leaves. Behind her, it was as if the hole she and Kai jumped through had vanished. In front of her was a strange and surreal world. Earthen walls led into a complex system of underground chambers and tunnels that seemed to travel on forever, maybe even to the other side of the earth.

Wynter let out a sigh of relief. She was protected from the derecho here. This refuge would offer her a haven until the storm passed.

"Hello. Is anyone here?" Wynter's voice echoed through the endless chambers.

"Back here," Wynter heard a soft voice respond.

Following the voice, Wynter entered a cooking chamber where she expected to see Kai, the magical hare. But instead of a hare, there was a breathtakingly beautiful auburn-haired fairy, cooking a meal over a slow burning fire.

Turning toward Wynter and being hospitable, Pumpkin Berry the fairy gently questioned, "May I share my food with you? I am always happy to prepare a meal for a tired and weary traveler."

"I would be grateful for that," Wynter shyly answered.

"Please make yourself at home," Pumpkin Berry said, pointing toward a table that was already set with table service for one.

Wynter took her seat at the table, mesmerized by the tiny fairy that busily buzzed around the fire.

"The simple act of sharing food has less to do with eating than with forming a friendship," Pumpkin Berry said, smiling.

"It's the essence of sharing the food that matters, not the substance of the food," the fairy continued.

The smiling fairy, the warm fire and the promise of a nourishing meal made Wynter feel relaxed and comfortable.

"Can you tell me where the hare is that I followed into this place?" Wynter questioned.

Pumpkin Berry flashed a smile at Wynter. "Didn't you know? We are one and the same."

"I'm not entirely sure I understand what you mean," Wynter replied.

"We are the same. We can appear here and there, now, and then, to this one or that one, but we are selective as to who we reveal ourselves to. You appeared to need our help. Even though you were quite far away, I could hear your thoughts." Pumpkin Berry smiled, offering Wynter a goblet filled with a drink called lambs-wool, made with milk and roasted apples.

"For dinner there is potatoes, parsnips, and onions," the fairy kindly said while filling Wynter's plate with food.

Wynter was hungrier than she realized. As she consumed the last bites of food from her plate, a round object unexpectedly scraped against her fork. Under the remaining food was a single coin.

Wynter abruptly stopped chewing and picked up the coin with her fingers, holding it up in the dim light.

"How can this be?" Wynter questioned the fairy.

But Wyner's question went unanswered as Pumpkin Berry continued buzzing around the cooking chamber.

"How can it be that there is a bright shiny coin is in my potatoes?" Wynter questioned Pumpkin Berry once again.

"On the night of Samhain, it is said that the one who finds a coin in their food will find abundance and prosperity in the coming days," Pumpkin Berry replied as she busily peeled apples for dessert.

"How did it get here?" Wynter said, suspiciously eyeing the coin that had mysteriously appeared in her food.

"Don't ask me. Maybe the wind blew it in," Pumpkin Berry replied with a grin as she returned to her apple peeling duties.

As the moon waxes and wanes
In the course of a year
Peaking then pausing to change
Set you intentions
Birth your dreams
To see what you may gain

Soul Friends

Wynter remained safe during the violent derecho, securely tucked away in Kai's sanctuary. The wind blew for nine consecutive days, masking the sound of everything except the violent wind itself.

After dinner that first night, Pumpkin Berry escorted Wynter to a comfortable, private sleeping chamber.

"Sleep well, Wynter," Pumpkin Berry whispered as Wynter drifted off to sleep.

The next morning when Wynter awoke, she slowly rose from her bed, remembering the previous evening. She walked down the long hallway that led to the cooking chamber where she had dined, but neither Kia nor Pumpkin Berry were there. Now they both seemed as elusive as a dream remembered upon waking and as mysterious as this timeless place.

During those next long, lonely days when night and day were the same, Wynter found herself reminiscing about the time she had spent with Sir Gyzmo, the canine hero, and Willow, the Shun, who stood only six inches tall. They had escorted Wynter through the Crooked Forest on the long trip to Snowdonia.

It had been Sir Gyzmo and Willow who discovered Wynter's tired and worn body slumped beside May Fae's well after she had fled from Aidan. Wynter had been aimlessly wandering through the forest for days before finding her way to May Fae's sacred well where she stopped to seek relief for her overburdened heart and the sorrow and despair that had worn her down.

Now Wynter was missing her soul friends and longed for their companionship. The strong and sturdy friendship they had formed was grounded in truthfulness and trust.

"Wouldn't it have been wonderful if my marriage to Aidan had been rooted in the same honesty as my friendships?" Wynter mused, reminded once again that forgiveness for Aidan could take all the time it needed to enter her heart, as forgiveness seemed to take hold in stages, vanishing at the most unexpected times.

This was one of those times.

By keeping his truth from Wynter, Aidan had acted from his ego and not from his heart. Really, he had put on a mask, becoming someone that he was not, then presented himself as that person to Wynter.

Aidan's ego had formed a protective crust between him and his beloved, costing him the purest and sweetest gift of his life.

For Wynter, living with a stranger had left her feeling isolated and lonely, as living in the shadow of the great question mark leaves worry, fear, and uncertainty in its path.

A reconciliation with Aidan was not in Wynter's future. Their relationship was damaged beyond repair. This insight arrived as suddenly and unexpectedly as the sound of shattered glass, as Wynter suddenly realized that she wasn't going back to New Leaf.

Change can be subtle or swift, but for Wynter, change was inevitable. The end of this tale was merely the beginning of another, and she was ready to move on.

Be mindful of your conduct
Don't cause your loved ones pain
Hurtful actions will not fade
Within the spirit plane

Samhain

It was the magical evening of Samhain, the cross-quarter point between the fall equinox and the winter solstice, now known as Halloween. The Crooked Forest was transformed with waves of magical silver mists that hung in the autumn air.

At dawn and at dusk on Samhain, the veil is exceptionally thin between the seen and the unseen worlds, making it the perfect time for omens and messages from the Otherworld to arrive since entities can move freely back and forth between the worlds during this time.

On Samhain, throngs of spirits, fairies, and goblins go out for merrymaking and could be seen trooping through the woods. The Crooked Forest was home to many supernatural beings, some who were known to trick travelers by leading them astray with flickering lights that led into another realms, resulting in lost time.

One might be lured by fairy music while stopping at a fairy fort to watch the fairies dancing. There is no one that can look upon the fairy dance and remain unaffected. Upon returning from such an event, one might find that the space of time which passed as merely one night, might have been three hundred years.

Aidan was feeling completely lost and miserable these days. Since Wynter's unexpected departure, all the color had vanished from his life, and he now saw everything in shades of black and gray. Likewise, he felt stark and gloomy, like a tree that has shed all its leaves and is left naked and unprotected.

To make matters worse, his flock of sheep had scattered in all directions during the derecho. He had scoured the countryside for days after the storm, managing to find only a few of them. Now their value had declined during these hard economic times, when one lamb equaled only a bushel of grain and wool had become useless.

The derecho had blown the roof from his home, and only minor renovations had been made to restore the damaged hut. Aidan sat at the table, his forehead resting in the palms of his hand. Raising his head, he brushed the gray strands of hair from his face as he looked up at the clock and awaited the stroke of the hour that marks the arrival of dusk. At long last, the clock struck, and Aidan gazed through the opening in his house where the door should be. Without speaking a word, he sat in his chair, shivering with fear, listening to the slow ticking clock chime.

Aidan's heart yearned for his lost love. Without the warmth of Wynter's love, there was no real possibility of celebration or enjoyment for Aidan.

As the wind howled through the leafless tree branches, Aidan feared an early and severe winter was ahead. Samhain marked the end of the harvest season and the beginning of the darker half of the year. That morning, Aidan had brought his flock down from the highlands, then he lit a special bonfire in hopes that the spirit world would protect his flock through winter.

Now Aidan hoped to connect with the otherworld on this Samhain night about his missing wife's whereabouts. Or just maybe his wife would return on her own.

There was a low mournful moaning sound that could have been anything or nothing as Aidan awaited the return of his long-lost love.

Pumpkin Berry Fairy

Pumpkin Berry had long auburn hair that was her crowning glory. She was as light as a bird and as slender as a reed, flying on invisible wings. Her green eyes flashed like lightning, and her voice was as lovely as a nightingale's song, entrancing all who heard her. Her pale skin was in dramatic contrast to the autumn-colored leaves that covered her tiny body.

Sent from above in the beginning days, Pumpkin Berry dropped through a hole in the sky, floating down through the atmosphere on an autumn breeze. Her descent to the middle world was slow and took time, as she journeyed through space, clutching in her hands a bundle containing seeds and plants of various kinds.

Upon her arrival in the Crooked Forest, she scattered the seeds and plants upon the ground, carefully tending them all until the earth turned green from her efforts.

She planted sweetgrass first, then flowers, and plants that flourished, their medicines offering natural cures for those who were trained in recognizing their healing remedies.

As Pumpkin Berry quietly landed in the field of sweetgrass that she had so tediously crafted so many centuries before, her thoughts turned to Wynter once again.

Unbeknownst to Wynter, Pumpkin Berry had been keeping a close eye on her. Peering through the sweetgrass and down the long lane that led to Old Mother Troll's dilapidated hut, Pumpkin Berry quietly kept watch. It wouldn't be long now. Wynter would arrive soon.

Old Mother Troll

Old Mother Troll had been living alone on her mountain for over three thousand years, and she was well versed in the medicinal remedies' nature offered. The mile long road that led to her cabin was lined with sweetgrass and her meager hut was surrounded by apple orchards, and hawthorn trees where mistletoe grew abundantly.

Wolves, bears, and foxes roamed freely through this region of the Crooked Forest and Old Mother Troll feasted on wolf chops and foxtail soup on a regular basis and bear ham was her favorite meal.

Recently, Old Mother Troll made a nighttime visit to the tiny nearby village of New Leaf. Stealthily, she had crept through the inky darkness of the forest to where the humans lived. Silently she entered their huts while they slept, never once waking them. From their closets she snatched their best clothing, then soundlessly, she exited through the same door she had entered, transporting the precious, stolen loot back to her hut.

The next morning the humans gathered, whispering about the mysterious disappearance of their finest garments. But no one recounted seeing or hearing anything out of the ordinary.

Back at her hut, Old Mother Troll tied a shawl over her matted, straggly hair to cover her face and conceal her bushy eyebrows and small black flashing eyes. Stroking the soft fabric of the satin ribbon she had snatched, she carefully tied up her tail, tucking it under her long skirt. The apron she had made off with, nicely fit around her generous waist and had two large, deep pockets where she could conceal her big hairy hands.

Sitting there in the darkest corner of her hut, old Mother Troll looked like a human as she rocked in her ancient rickety rocker. Opening the Book the Wisdom to a well ear-marked page, she situated a pair of stolen glasses on her large turnip shaped nose and began to recite an old troll rhyme.

> What I know is what I see
> And what I see stays with me
> Where are you Wynter
> so sweet and so dear
> I'm looking for you everywhere

Abruptly, Old Mother Troll stopped rocking, peering through a single dingy window, up at the circles of light that appeared in the sky exactly as she spoke the rhyme. Within the circle, Pumpkin Berry danced, before lightly descending into the sweet smelling sweetgrass that surrounded the ancient troll home.

"I'm not calling for you, Pumpkin Berry," Old Mother Troll grumbled, looking up at the circles of light. "Pesky fairy!"

"Leave me be. Can't you see I've got business to conduct?" Old Mother Troll grunted as she commenced rocking, the creak of her rocking chair echoing through her tiny hut. Her gaze fell upon a dusty shelf lined with a mysterious collection of different colored glass bottles filled with various liquids, powders, and herbs that she used in the concoctions she sold whenever the opportunity arose.

The leaves and berries of the mistletoe that covered Old Mother Troll's Hawthorn trees contained great power, and the top-secret love and healing potions she created from them were famous throughout the forest.

Old Mother Troll would grind the leaves with her ancient mortar and pestle to craft sedatives and nerve tonics. She was mostly known for her True Love Powder, and it was rumored that her copy of the Book of Wisdom contained the recipe for crafting mistletoe wands that could be used to unlock the gates between the realms of the worlds.

It was during the time of the waning moon, that special time before the reappearance of the crescent moon, that Old Mother Troll mixed up her magic. She believed that all physical objects contained energy and that the divine spark of creation dwelled within the crystals, stones, herbs, and feathers she worked with.

Under complete darkness, Old Mother Troll mixed the yellow flowers of cowslip with vervain and mistletoe berries, stirring them all together to create potions, boiling them in her ancient cauldron over a slow burning fire.

Old Mother Troll's love of bright shiny coins was the driving force behind her potion business. Knowing that some beings feared trolls, she disguised herself as a human by wearing clothing. It wasn't at all considered odd for humans to sell a variety of items, so old Mother Troll presented herself as a human so she wouldn't be feared, and she could collect more of the bright shiny coins she loved so much.

Over time she collected so many bags of coins that her hut was no longer big enough to house them. So she decided to build an additional structure. Digging first through the side of a hill, then carefully laying one stone at a time, she constructed a storage chamber. The entrance doorway aligned with the sunset on the winter solstice. Inside, the stone walls were covered with pictures of lunar calendars that depicted the passing of time, and ancient prayers that honored the cycles of nature.

Bags of roots and herbs and sacks of bright shiny coins were protected here in this craftily constructed chamber, where the intense magnetic pull in front of the entry was strong enough to reverse a compass and drive away any unwanted visitors.

Once again Old Mother Troll ceased her rocking, intuitively sensing that someone or something had just stepped onto her property. Her big mouth widened into a smile showing off her large green teeth.

"She's arrived." Old Mother Troll cackled as she closed her eyes to *see* the beautiful Wynter stepping onto the mile-long road that led to Old Mother Troll's dilapidated hut.

Owl Medicine

When the derecho ended, Wynter left her hiding place behind, as the same hole in the earth where she had entered mysteriously opened, providing her a safe exit.

She traveled through the forest for two days without encountering another living being, but on the third day, she detected the smell of smoke coming from the chimney stack of a dilapidated hut at the end of a long lane. Someone was living there.

Wynter had no idea that Old Mother Troll was expecting her.

Approaching the hut, Wynter peeked through a small dingy window to see an old woman in a rocker, reading from a book, with a shawl pulled tightly around her head.

Seeing Wynter through the window, the old troll who was disguised as a woman, rose from her rocking chair, taking the two steps needed to reach the entry and open the creaky door that hung cockeyed from its rusty hinges and moaned when opened.

"Can I help you, dear?" the old troll crooned.

"Maybe," Wynter replied. "I could use a place to spend the night if you have room, Mom. I'm on my way to begin my new life, but I could use a rest tonight."

Old Mother Troll smiled coyly, careful not to show her green teeth to her visitor.

"Of course, my dear. Come in here with me," Old Mother Troll said as she stepped back to allow Wynter into her tiny space.

"I have a nice bed made of soft moss and leaves to offer you," Old Mother Troll said, careful to keep her large furry hands concealed in her pockets as she glanced toward the offered bed.

"Thank you. This will do just fine," Wynter said as she sat down upon the soft bed.

Wynter cocked her head, taking a closer look at the old woman. "There is something I am looking for help with. You appear to be of the age to have the wisdom of the old traditions, Mom. Maybe you can help me."

"My true age remains a mystery even to me." Old Mother Troll sighed as she dropped back into her rocking chair, carefully keeping her long skirt pulled close to conceal her tail.

"Is it possible that you've come for my True Love Potion? You are of the perfect age to experience the magic of love," Old Mother Troll suggested.

"No, I don't think so. I would be more interested in learning the skill of perceiving deception. Can you help me with that?" Wynter boldly questioned.

Old Mother Troll rocked in her chair and slyly smiled through her long green teeth. "Of course, dear. The medicine of the owl identifies deception. He can teach you to decipher information with pitch-perfect observation."

"When I was a child, I had a companion owl that rode on my shoulder. The owl taught me how to identify the whole truth as opposed to half-truths. I learned much from the owl and so can you," Old Mother Troll stated.

"If you would care to stay awhile you are welcome to," Old Mother Troll plotted, "I still have the power to summon the owl if I wish. Of course, I would need to charge you a small fee for my services."

Wynter suddenly remembered the bright shiny coin that had mysteriously appeared in her food on the night of Samhain.

"Will this be sufficient compensation? It is the only coin I have," Wynter questioned, offering the coin to the troll.

"That will do splendidly!" Old Mother Troll's eyes lit up as she focused on the bright shiny coin, snatching it quickly from Wynter's fingers.

"Now that our business is done, we can make plans to begin your training. How does first thing in the morning sound?" Old Mother Troll questioned.

"In the morning will be fine," Wynter answered. "How long do you expect it will take?"

Old Mother Troll peered craftily from under her shawl. "It will take as long as it takes. When you see, you will know, and when you know, then you will see."

Bright and early the next morning, Old Mother Troll summoned the owl and Wynter's training began. Old Mother Troll, Wynter, and the owl worked together for some time, until Wynter possessed the power to summon the owl herself.

It was then that Wynter travelled on from Old Mother Trolls hut in search of a place to begin her new life.

During those days, stories began to circulate among the forest beings of Wynter and the owl being seen together, silently working, the owl educating the student.

The owl taught Wynter how to detect deception through a place of silence and observation, and her reputation grew legendary as she learned to identify tricksters and any who sought to use her as a resource for their own personal gain or selfish ego. Within Wynter the owl medicine grew strong, and many became nervous in her presence because she now had the power to perceive any attempt at deception with a hunter's vigilance.

Remedies

Much time had passed since the day when Luna stepped effortlessly through the invisible border that led her into the Otherworld. Luna was a Shun, or little person, who lived in the mysterious Crooked Forest—a place where deep wells imparted forgotten wisdom and gates opened into secret passages, leading to strange realms.

While in the Otherworld, Luna was offered the rest her physically worn body required to heal, and over time she became renewed and rejuvenated and she felt capable of resuming life on the earth plane once more.

Just before ascending into the Otherworld, Luna experienced a traumatic event when Aidan, the human sheepherder, caught her gathering the mistletoe herb, which she regularly harvested for use in treating her frequent headaches. But gathering herbs of any kind had been outlawed by the humans, and Aidan aimed to uphold that law at all costs.

"These Shuns never learn," Aidan grumbled to himself as he pulled out a handful of stones from his pocket and hurled them at his tiny target. But Luna stood only six inches tall, so the stones that sailed through the air missed her entirely as she raced through the forest to escape.

"There's no tolerance for hocus pocus in my forest!" Aidan yelled as he chased after Luna for miles before losing her trail and tragically separating her from her daughter, Willow, who was silently observing as the tragic event unfolded.

Terrified, Willow braced herself against the base of a crooked pine tree for support, placing one hand on her forehead and one hand on her heart. Feeling tightness in her chest and pounding in her temple, she closed her eyes until the dizziness passed. Willow was experiencing broken heart syndrome, a condition that can be brought on by experiencing an overwhelming tragedy or sudden shock.

Later that same night, drained from her harrowing experience with Aidan, Luna sought refuge inside a fantastically large, crooked pine tree. The next morning, Luna left the warm nest inside the tree hole, her legs still trembling with exhaust as she weakly lowered herself to the ground.

Directly before her was what appeared to be a ceremonial pathway. Luna's legs quivered and shook as she stepped toward the ancient portal that was topped with a heavy horizontal capstone. She felt nauseated as she fell through the boundaries where the veil was thin, landing her in the Otherworld.

Eventually, Luna was reunited with her daughter, Willow, who had grown into a heroine during her mother's absence. And she was introduced to Sir Gyzmo, the canine champion, who had magically appeared the same day as Luna's and Willow's heartbreaking separation, saving Willow from complete and total despair.

Now, Luna, Willow, and Sir Gyzmo lived together as a family in this intensely magical place where the portal stones were aligned with the sunrise of the summer solstice.

But the path of destruction left by the mighty derecho ran far and wide, and even the landscape of this supernatural area was changed in a way that presented new challenges for the tight-knit family unit. The derecho had carried the mistletoe herb far away from where it once thrived. The plant that magically attaches itself to tree branches, mysteriously growing suspended between heaven and earth, had vanished. Now the forest was void of the mystical herb that was known as the most valuable plant in nature, proven to cure disease, make poisons harmless, and bring good luck.

Without mistletoe, Luna's headaches worsened and eventually became debilitating. Now she was unable to perform even the simplest of her daily tasks, and Willow and Sir Gyzmo were becoming more and more worried about her declining condition.

Willow began to fear that her mother would not recover, and soon her heart began to ache with an old familiar pain. Only recently had she been reunited with Luna, and now with Sir Gyzmo, they were a family. It was all she had dreamed of during their separation and now the future of her family was in jeopardy.

Gathering foliage and soft moss, Willow and Sir Gyzmo made Luna a comfortable, warm bed where she could rest. They kept a small fire going around the clock to keep their patient warm. Willow made broth from the local vegetation and patiently hand fed her mother small amounts of the hot liquid throughout the day.

"I fear she won't recover," Willow whispered to Sir Gyzmo as they kept vigil at Luna's side.

Lately the urge to cry came on at any second, and Willow was filled with feelings of desperation and fear that her mother might not recover.

"I must embark upon a search for a remedy," Sir Gyzmo began as he carefully began to lay out his plan.

"I will travel outside the boundaries of the storm's destruction zone to find a place where mistletoe still grows, however far that turns out to be," Sir Gyzmo stated bravely, as only a true hero would.

"You can't go alone. It's far too dangerous for you to travel that far away without me!" Willow cried, knowing that this would be the first time she would be separated from Sir Gyzmo since the very first day when they had met.

"I have no choice, my family is in jeopardy," Sir Gyzmo valiantly replied.

"You must stay here to care for Luna, and I will be back before you know it," Sir Gyzmo continued. And in an instant, the canine hero was gone.

Shadow Figures

The solitary tree grew alone within the shadowy forest, one singular looking branch extending horizontally from its ancient trunk, resembling an elongated arm with its boney hand outstretched and its fingers widespread and crooked, the sacred mistletoe plant extending from its branches.

Within her dream, Luna saw herself sleeping soundly under the tree as the branch's arm and hand began to descend, its fingers outstretched and ready to envelope her in its icy grip.

Paralyzed by fear, Luna watched as the eerie arm descended lower and lower until its gnarly hand hovered only inches above her face and the tips of the long fingers grazed her sleeping form.

As if she were outside her own body. Luna saw herself reach for the mistletoe plant that grew from the tree's arm, but it escaped her. Time and time again she lunged to grab the plant with no success.

In the next seconds, the fingers changed and became soft as satin, closing over her nose and mouth.

Luna awoke from her nightmare shrieking with fear. The sacred mistletoe plant had escaped her once again.

Luna's scream woke Willow from her own fitful sleep. Bolting upright, Willow was immediately filled with a feeling of trepidation. Since the cross-quarter day known as Samhain, Willow had been feeling increasingly uneasy as Luna's health declined.

The easy days of summer had passed as quickly as a single breath, and Willow was acutely aware of the fading light that comes with the approach of the winter solstice.

It is a frightening thing to love what sickness touches. The air surrounding Willow and Luna was thick with grief and heavy like water. Willow felt that heaviness in her shoulders as she slumped beside Luna's trembling form.

She simply could not lose her mother.

I built a special place
In the corner of my heart
Keeping faith that you'll be safe
Please stay and don't depart

In this space the music plays
And the flowers smell so sweet
It's where I want to spend my days
As long as your heart beats

Where Angels Live

At sunrise, Luna fell back to sleep. Willow sat on the bank of Sleeping Creek, quietly sobbing as she grieved the loss of the optimistic plans she had made for the future of her beloved family unit. Luna's condition had deteriorated since Sir Gyzmo's departure, and she was becoming weaker with each passing day.

The sound of Luna's labored breathing was the only thing Willow could hear within the forest, amplifying the loneliness she felt inside her heart without the constant companionship of her best friend and canine hero, Sir Gyzmo.

Willow and Sir Gyzmo had carefully selected this healing location due to its proximity to Sleeping Creek. In the quiet moments while Luna slept, Willow would sit by the edge of Sleeping Creek, finally allowing the grief she held in her heart to escape. Sobs wracked her tiny body and tears spilled from her eyes and down her face, feeling as though they would never cease.

She was beginning to feel physically worn down. Wiping the tears from her face with her tiny hand, she unexpectedly caught a glimpse of herself in the clear water's reflection. She was shocked to see her worn expression and swollen eyes and face.

"Willow?" she heard her mother murmur as she immediately returned to Luna's side.

"What do you need, Mama?" Willow tenderly asked, kneeling beside her mother.

Weakly Luna reached up to touch her daughter's face.

"I look dreadful," Willow said sadly.

"I just saw my reflection in the water's reflection, and I hardly recognize myself. What's wrong with my face, Mama? I don't look the same," Willow asked as her fingers touched the puffy swollen pockets that had appeared under her eyes.

"Angels live there," Luna whispered weakly."

"I see a face that is so beautiful that it must be inhabited by angels. That's what I see when I look at you, Willow," Luna so poetically conveyed before drifting off once more to sleep.

The Presence of a Hero

He felt the owl silently approach, flying over his head, producing a slight rustling—that was the sound of the owl's feathers moving through the air.

If there had been any doubt about which way to go, there wasn't now, as Sir Gyzmo followed the owl up a mile long road lined with sweetgrass and apple trees. He passed by a ramshackle hut, following the sound of a whispered chant that he couldn't quite identify, feeling that this place was so intensely magical that anything might happen.

Old Mother Troll was busily building a fire under her pewter cauldron that was filled with the magical water of Sleeping Creek. The whispered chant Sir Gyzmo overheard was the voice of Old Mother Troll as she spoke to the stones that lined her firepit. She referred to them as the bones of the earth, and she held them in high regard as they contained the wisdom of nature since the beginning of time.

Sir Gyzmo gazed at the startling figure of Old Mother Troll who had begun sprinkling valerian sprigs and roots into the boiling water of her cauldron, creating her secret nerve tonic. Her straggly hair had come unpinned and stuck out from under the shawl she had pulled tightly over her head and tied under her chin. Sir Gyzmo watched silently as her tail switched back and forth, visible from under her skirt as she stirred the brew with a long stick grasped in her big furry hands.

Sir Gyzmo needed mistletoe, and trolls always knew the pathways that lead over and under the hills of the forest. *Maybe this one will help me,* Sir Gyzmo thought as he observed the troll's magical mistletoe wand sticking out of her apron pocket. That wand could unlock the entrance into and out of the Otherworld with ease.

He wondered if he could trust her. Usually, female trolls are wise women and keepers of home and hearth.

Usually.

Perched upon a scraggly limb of an ancient Hawthorne tree sat the owl that Sir Gyzmo had encountered earlier. His keen yellow eyes all but looked through Sir Gyzmo as he suddenly relocated, landing upon Old Mother Trolls bent and bony shoulder.

Old Mother Troll grinned wide, showing all her green sharp teeth to the owl who was her trusted friend.

"Of course, I know that he has arrived." She crooned lovingly to the owl.

"Don't you think I would immediately know that I was in the presence of a hero?" She cackled, turning to face Sir Gyzmo, her finely tuned intuition once again on point.

A Bright Shiny Coin

"We've been waiting for your arrival," Old Mother Troll said casually as she nodded toward her trusted friend, the owl, who remained settled upon her shoulder. The owl's golden, unblinking eyes peered hungrily at Sir Gyzmo as if the small dog might make a light and tasty snack.

"Your reputation as a hero precedes you, Sir Gyzmo. We've heard the legends concerning your noble qualities and heroism. I'm always happy to assist a hero. You're here for a remedy, I presume," Old Mother Troll stated as she turned toward the simmering cauldron to resume concocting the potion she brewed.

"I am," Sir Gyzmo replied, stepping closer to the troll.

"I'm in urgent need of mistletoe herb. Luna is suffering without it. The area where we live and all the forests around there are void of mistletoe since the derecho blew through. Without mistletoe, Luna will not recover. She is becoming weaker by the day."

Old Mother Troll coyly peered from under her big, bushy eyebrows. "Of course, I can help you. I have a nice selection of mistletoe to offer you as well as my famous tonics and true love potions."

"I would be forever grateful for your help," Sir Gyzmo replied.

"Certainly. But I will need to charge you a small fee in exchange for my help." Old Mother Troll grinned.

"A fee? What kind of fee?" Sir Gyzmo asked.

"Why, a fee for my service of course. One bright shiny coin will buy you all the mistletoe you can carry back home to Luna," Old Mother Troll schemed.

"Sadly, I don't have a coin," Sir Gyzmo responded.

"That's unfortunate. It seems to me that every hero should have at least a single coin. No coin, no mistletoe," Old Mother Troll replied sharply.

"Won't you consider some other form of payment?" Sir Gyzmo questioned.

"I said, no coin, no mistletoe," the troll repeated.

"Maybe I could be of some help around here by providing a service to you in exchange for the mistletoe I so desperately need. Possibly there are some chores that I could assist with," Sir Gyzmo offered.

Old Mother Troll frowned at Sir Gyzmo. "I've lived in this same spot for over three thousand years. What makes you think I would need your help with anything around here, little dog?" Old Mother Troll said condescendingly.

Sir Gyzmo was not deterred. "My family's future depends on me returning with mistletoe. Can't we reach some kind of agreement that doesn't involve the exchange of coins?"

"Your family is not my concern," Old Mother Troll replied coldly. "And the only way your family will become my concern is when you return here with a bright, shiny coin. Until then, be gone, little dog."

The yellow-eyed owl watched as Sir Gyzmo prepared to leave, then flew over him, escorting him all the way to the end of the lane. Sir Gyzmo never looked back at the owl or at Old Mother Troll's property. He was on a quest for mistletoe, so he bravely carried on, entering an entirely different zone of the forest; one he had never journeyed through before.

The Green Man

The Green Man was born from the tree of life and was considered the king of the forest and sometimes referred to as the wild man of the woods.

He had green hair and brown skin, and his form was covered in foliage. His duty was to keep the woods wild and provide a sanctuary for the plants, trees, rivers, and animals. He possessed the magical ability to produce a portal through which he could hear, see, communicate, and transport himself when necessary.

The Green Man lived in the shadow lands of the Crooked Forest, where he remained hidden and rarely seen. Any place in nature that is neither one place nor another belongs to another realm and the upside-down trees marking the boundary between Old Mother Troll's property and the Green Man's home was one of those betwixt and between places.

It was said that the Green Man could be seen in the betwixt and between times, like dawn or dusk, which is neither daytime nor nighttime. Or at noon which is neither morning nor afternoon, or midnight which is neither one day nor the next. But one thing was for certain. One could never be truly prepared for a magical encounter with the Green Man.

Upside Down Trees

It was just moments before dawn. Sir Gyzmo had travelled far from Old Mother Troll's property without finding mistletoe. Now, he had arrived in an odd part of the forest where the trees appeared to have been plucked from the ground and flipped upside down, their roots now facing skyward, where once they had been buried five feet deep in the ground.

Cautiously he continued, passing by the peculiar identifiers that marked the exit from one space into another. Where some might consider these trees that seemed to defy gravity a marker of evil, Sir Gyzmo saw their appearance as a reminder that while all life is rooted in the earth, any being's roots could reach as high as the heavens.

Sir Gyzmo stopped, seeing a clearing before him. There stood two giant Hawthorne trees that had twisted together at their base to become one. Its simple beauty and strength mesmerized Sir Gyzmo. As he continued to stare at the tree, the lines in the bark began to subtly change and shift, as a pair of soft, gentle eyes peered out from the bark, meeting Sir Gyzmo's gaze. Sir Gyzmo was no longer watching the tree; the tree was watching him.

As the orange rays of sunshine filled the perfectly blue sky, there was a mysterious movement and a form stepped from the sturdy tree, standing in its own shadow. Around the Green Man, tiny lights flickered, and Sir Gyzmo knew the lights were the Moss People who lived at the base of the tree in the root system. They were stern upholders of the old ways, and they possessed the secret location of the blue flower, Ache-no-more.

Cowslip, foxgloves, and thyme grew thick around the base of the Green Man's tree. The wildflowers and the Moss People sharing in the protective energy surrounding the Green Man.

The leaves of the tree rustled as the Green Man spoke Sir Gyzmo's name.

Sir Gyzmo had not allowed himself to think about just how exhausted he truly was. He heard the Green Man speak his name again and he slumped to the ground.

Lying on the ground and looking up into the top of tree, Sir Gyzmo saw mistletoe abundantly growing from the tree's mighty branches. The Hawthorne tree where mistletoe grows is considered the most magical and powerful of all the trees in the forest. Where the mistletoe clung, the Moss People danced, their lights flickering as if to aid those that are pure of heart like Sir Gyzmo.

As the tiny lights twinkled and danced around the fairy dog, Sir Gyzmo closed his eyes, hearing his name spoken again. He had reached his destination. He couldn't move from where he lay. He simply couldn't muster the energy to stand, and yet he had never felt safer as he gently closed his eyes.

Second Sight

It had been a long and difficult night for Luna and Willow. Luna had been calling out in her sleep throughout the night, and Willow had been unable to bring her mother any comfort or relief. Luna's fever had spiked at midnight, and now that dawn was breaking, her fever seemed to be breaking as well.

In last night's fitful dream, Luna saw herself standing beneath two giant hawthorn trees that had twisted together at the base and now grew as one. The tree's bark was twisted and gnarled, and the tree's roots were exposed and were so large they appeared to reach into the middle of the earth.

Looking up from beneath the tree branches, Luna felt small but safe. It was if the branches had formed a dome of protection between her and the outside world.

A soft mist began to form on the ground, and the grass became hidden from view along with the base of the tree. Only dim light entered through the thickening mist as it rose to meet the tree branches.

"Is it day or night?" Luna thought to herself as the mist closed around her, leaving a fragrance behind as sweet as honeysuckle.

The mist began to swirl around Luna, and she saw a face and a figure form within the tree.

"Green Man," Luna whispered, and the mist responded by shifting and dancing and the figure form became clearly defined.

"Green Man," Luna spoke a second time, this time louder and more confidently.

The mist swirled around the base of the tree and the figure began to move as if it could walk right out of the tree.

"Green Man," Luna called out a third time from her restless sleep as the mist parted, and the Green Man stepped right out of the ancient tree.

New Starts

After months of traveling, Wynter found herself at the betwixt and between place once again. She had traveled with the wise owl over many moon cycles and learned the lessons of identifying deception. Her senses were now razor sharp when confronted with an untruth, and she felt safe from the fear of being deceived again.

She had survived the derecho by spending nine days underground in Kia's den. A fine meal had been prepared for her by the air elemental, Pumpkin Berry, who just happened to leave her the exact thing she required to make training with the owl possible. One bright, shiny coin had mysteriously appeared in her food just as the magical night of Samhain arrived. That single coin had obtained the owl's services from Old Mother Troll who never performed favors without the exchange of coins. Her time spent with the owl left Wynter with a new sense of hope for the future, a feeling that had been absent from her life for a while.

Just ahead was a high mountain and a path leading up to it lined with ancient ceremonial stones. This place felt familiar to Wynter as if she somehow already knew of it or had seen it before. Maybe she had seen it in her dreams, maybe she was remembering it from a distant lifetime. It didn't matter.

"Wynter," she heard her name called, although she did not know the source of the voice. What she did know was that the pathway before her led to her new home.

When the heart stops beating
The sound of the beat remains
Leaving a bit of oneself behind
Before entering the spirit plane

From the Mist

The mist slowly began to dissipate, and Luna abruptly woke from her dream state to see Willow's worried face. It had been an incredibly long night for Willow, as she watched over Luna, and the strain showed clearly.

Luna moved her head from side to side, attempting to get her bearings. From the corner of her eye, she detected movement near the trees surrounding her resting place.

The Green Man was carefully laying Sir Gyzmo's worn and exhausted form upon the ground. Next, he produced an abundant bundle of mistletoe, which he laid beside the motionless puppy.

Luna focused her eyes only to see the Green Man step back into the tree, disappearing just as quickly as he had appeared. Too weak and confused to speak, Luna raised her hand slightly and silently pointed.

Willow followed the direction of Luna's pointing finger to see Sir Gyzmo's lifeless body lying on the ground. Jumping up, she ran toward her trusted companion.

"Sir Gyzmo!" Willow cried kneeling beside the puppy. "You can't leave me, I need you."

As Willow stroked the soft fur around Sir Gyzmo's ears, he began to stir ever so slowly. It was as if he had just awoken from a very deep sleep, yet he couldn't remember how he had gotten home.

"What happened? Are you alright?" Willow questioned.

Sir Gyzmo seemed dazed as he struggled to stand, his legs feeling incredibly weak and wobbly.

"The last thing I remember is entering the place where the upside-down trees grow. I saw the image of a man stepping out from the inside of a tree, and that is the last thing I remember," Sir Gyzmo recollected.

"The Green Man," Luna whispered. "You saw the Green Man. I saw him too. I thought I was having a dream, but he was here!"

"And you found mistletoe!" Luna exclaimed.

Sir Gyzmo looked at the heaping stack of the precious herb. "I remember now. It was the last thing I saw before I collapsed. The Green Man stepped from a giant tree that had more mistletoe growing on it than I have ever seen."

Willow hastily fetched a kettle and filled it full of water. Grabbing the precious mistletoe, she began to prepare the herb for brewing the medicinal tea that would surely cure Luna and return her to a healthy state.

A Child's Eye

"Look at them playing together. They are so beautiful!" Wynter said to Luna as they sat together, happily watching as Sir Gyzmo and Willow played.

From clay, Willow had created a small bronze pendant in the shape of Sir Gyzmo. The amulet had a long-elongated body, delicate snout, and accentuated ears. At the top of the amulet where the corgi fairy saddle was located, she had added a small ring for hanging the piece around her neck. Sir Gyzmo sat close to Willow as she busily crafted a chain made from coyote willows so that she could wear her precious creation as a necklace.

"They are my heart," Luna replied, her chest swelling with pride.

"When I met them, I was at the lowest point of my life. I had been wandering the woods in a state of shock after learning who my husband truly was. I don't know what would have become of me had they not found me beside May Fae's sacred well," Wynter winced.

"They helped me when I needed true friends. Even though they had never met me, they didn't hesitate to pause their lives and escort me to Snowdonia, teaching me all about the natural world and nature's remedies along the way. The knowledge I received from them enabled me to perform the one year and one day long ritual, and I thought of them daily during my seclusion. I'm not sure I can truly express the gratitude and thankfulness I feel for their friendship," Wynter continued.

"You being here to share in this beautiful moment in time is thanks enough dear Wynter. And going forward, we would like to help you in any way we can. That's our purpose here on earth, isn't it? To support each other and the greater good that will be of benefit to all beings," Luna asked.

Wynter wiped a tear from her eye and forced a smile. "Once upon a time I was joyful like your Willow is. I thought everyone that I met could be a possible new friend and I had a positive attitude and trusted most everyone. My heart had not yet been wounded and I looked at the world through the eyes of a child. But I was a naive girl, and not very savvy in the ways of the world and people in general. I took it for granted that people will do the right thing and be honest and trustworthy. Now, I am forever changed. Because of my failed marriage, I've lost faith in love." Wynter sighed.

"You are not alone, Wynter. I have experienced the grief of not meaning all that much to one I freely gave the best of myself to," Luna said wistfully.

"Like you, I was young when I first met and fell in love with Willow's birth father, Ceri. But Ceri's family treasured him in what most of the world would consider an unnatural way. His parents and siblings became irritated and jealous when he and I spent time together, and they voiced their disdain loudly, hoping to strike discord in our relationship. Their arrogance was so strong that Ceri couldn't rail against it. He didn't possess the courage needed to speak up for us, so he remained silent," Luna continued.

"The truth was that it stoked his ego to be put upon such a high pedestal, and he relished the adoration he received from his family. I finally realized that I would never truly hold his heart and I was coming between the sturdy blood bonds of his tight knit family," Luna concluded.

Wynter's mouth dropped open with surprise. "Do you ever wish things had turned out differently?"

"Broken love can be like broken glass. You will only hurt yourself trying to put the broken pieces back together," Luna stated.

"Our parting wasn't the end of my story, it was simply the end of his part in my story. Over time I realized that even the most painful experiences can yield cherished miracles. As a result of my bond with Ceri, Willow was born, and she is the greatest gift of my life," Luna said smiling.

Wynter smiled wistfully at Willow who was wearing her new necklace while Sir Gyzmo chased after her, barking all the while.

"I am eternally grateful to Sir Gyzmo for saving Willow from complete despair. She suffered a broken heart during our separation. I feared she would not recover from the trauma of seeing Aidan hurl rocks at me and chase after me, screaming all the while. I was lucky to survive," Luna continued, a faraway look in her eye as she recalled that tragic day.

"Sir Gyzmo is a true hero, and I am happy to call him a part of my family. I don't believe that family is limited by blood ties. It is quite possible to find a strong sense of unity with others outside our blood relations. I believe that Shuns, humans, and even canine heroes can all be a unit. That's why I would like to ask you to stay here with us Wynter and become a part of our family," Luna proposed.

Wynter's heart expanded as she heard the welcoming words. There was nothing she would have liked more.

"When I saw the path leading here, I got the undeniable feeling that I was coming home," Wynter shared.

"We can create whatever life we want for ourselves," Luna began. "The earth is the blank canvas nature provides and the background for the journey and the life we endeavor to create for ourselves. Stay here with us. I think it is meant to be, considering the way our lives have intertwined like vines to create our unique storylines.

"Our story is certainly not one that could have been fabricated." Wynter chuckled.

"Certainly not!" Luna laughed. "Do you think it was just a coincidence that I was chased relentlessly through the forest by a man that you would later marry? Or that it was just blind luck that you were rescued by my daughter and Sir Gyzmo in your most desperate moment? Who else could have taught you the laws of nature in a way that served you so well? And after all of us survived the derecho, we just happen to find ourselves together once again?"

"It sure doesn't sound like any coincidence to me." Wynter grinned.

"It's fate," Luna said, smiling.

And it came to pass over their lives, that Luna, Willow, Wynter, and Sir Gyzmo became a family unit. Their commitment to each other was not limited by blood ties. They were joined in an ancient and eternal way because of freely giving their hearts to each other.

Their passion for life left an indelible mark on all beings they encountered within the Crooked Forest, and the positivity of their actions left the forest a better place.

Mother, daughter, spirit guide, companion, and teacher, they were all these things to each other; but above all, they were soul friends. A bond so strong that it can never be destroyed or severed.

Over the years they shared many happy times together, but time has a way of making a ghost of all our experiences. Every dawn fades to afternoon, and every afternoon fades to evening. Days will vanish, disappearing forever into a place called memory that exists within us all.

Within their family unit an ancient circle had closed around them. There was a feeling of belonging that held them together. Even in death, the love they shared for each other was remembered and those memories became legend, leaving their imprint upon the Crooked Forest for generations to come.

Until we meet again.

Printed in the United States
by Baker & Taylor Publisher Services